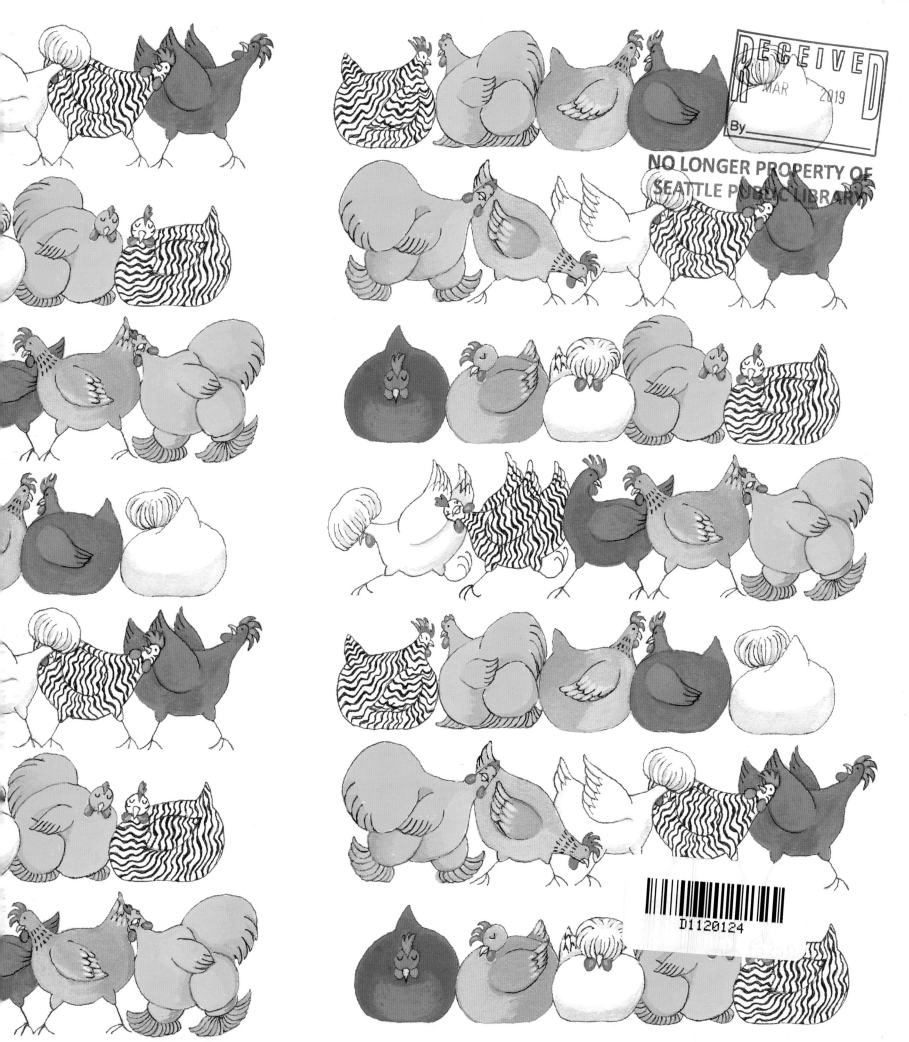

In memory of Roberta Pressel

Farrar Straus Giroux Books for Young Readers
An imprint of Macmillan Publishing Group, LLC
175 Fifth Avenue, New York, NY 10010

Copyright © 2019 by Barbara Samuels
All rights reserved
Printed in China by RR Donnelley Asia Printing Solutions Ltd.,
Dongguan City, Guangdong Province
Designed by Roberta Pressel
First edition, 2019
1   3   5   7   9   10   8   6   4   2

mackids.com

Library of Congress Cataloging-in-Publication Data

Names: Samuels, Barbara, author, illustrator.
Title: The chickens are coming! / Barbara Samuels.
Description: First edition. | New York : Farrar Straus Giroux, 2019. |
    Summary: Sophie and Winston are excited about raising chickens in their
    backyard in the city, but when will there be eggs?
Identifiers: LCCN 2018018314 | ISBN 9780374300975 (hardcover)
Subjects: | CYAC: Brothers and sisters—Fiction. | Chickens—Fiction. |
    Eggs—Fiction. | City and town life—Fiction.
Classification: LCC PZ7.S1925 Chi 2019 | DDC [E]—dc23
LC record available at https://lccn.loc.gov/2018018314

Our books may be purchased in bulk for promotional, educational, or business use.
Please contact your local bookseller or the Macmillan Corporate and Premium Sales Department
at (800) 221-7945 ext. 5442 or by email at MacmillanSpecialMarkets@macmillan.com.

Dawn

Desirée

Divina

The CHICKENS Are COMING!

Delilah

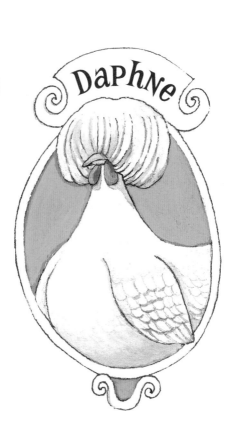

Daphne

Barbara Samuels

Farrar Straus Giroux ⬮ New York

One day Mommy, Winston, and Sophie saw
an interesting sign:

"You don't need to live in the country to raise chickens!" said Mommy. "We have a backyard— the chickens can come live with us!"

"Chickens make good pets!" Daddy said.

And Sophie said, "Chickens are better than dogs. They know how to lay eggs."

"I want to walk a chicken," said Winston.

"**Nobody** walks a chicken!" said Sophie.

"The chickens are coming soon," said Sophie.

"I'll give each of you an egg at the next show-and-tell."

"THE CHICKENS ARE COMING TOMORROW!" Winston told everyone on the bus. Then he did the Chicken Dance.

"THE CHICKENS ARE HERE!"

Their names were Desirée, Daphne, Divina, Delilah, and Dawn.

"I like the one with the hat!" said Winston.
"Chickens don't wear hats!" said Sophie. "That's the way Daphne's feathers grow."

Winston introduced himself: "Hi, my name is Winston!

"I like pizza with pepperoni, and my favorite TV show is

"The Deep-Sea Adventures of a Lobster Named Leonard!"

The next day Winston and Sophie went out with
their baskets to collect the eggs.

There were no eggs, but there
was plenty of chicken poop!

Three days later—still not a **SINGLE** egg. All the chickens did was roll in the dirt. Daddy said they were taking dirt baths to help get rid of bugs.

The chickens weren't the only ones who liked dirt baths.

"**You** are not a chicken!" said Mommy.

A week went by—**NO EGGS YET!**
Something had to be done. Sophie and
Winston put on a play.

The chickens were more
interested in leftover linguine
and stale bagels.

Daddy said music helps chickens lay eggs. Sophie played her violin for them.

BRRAANG!

Winston played his guitar.

STILL NO EGGS!

The next night, Winston read the chickens a special bedtime story to get them in the mood.

It didn't.

But every day as the children watched
the chickens, they learned more about them:

Desirée was the best flier.

Delilah was the most curious.

Divina was bossy. Dawn was shy.

And Daphne bumped into things.

Soon, Winston and Sophie were spending much of their time

hanging out with Desirée,

doing homework with Delilah,

Stop it, Divina!

keeping Divina from bullying Dawn,

and telling secrets to Daphne.

One morning, they heard a big commotion coming from the coop.

Buk-buk bawk!

Sophie grabbed her chicken chart and she and Winston rushed out to the backyard.

And there it was, the very first egg! It was **PERFECT**...

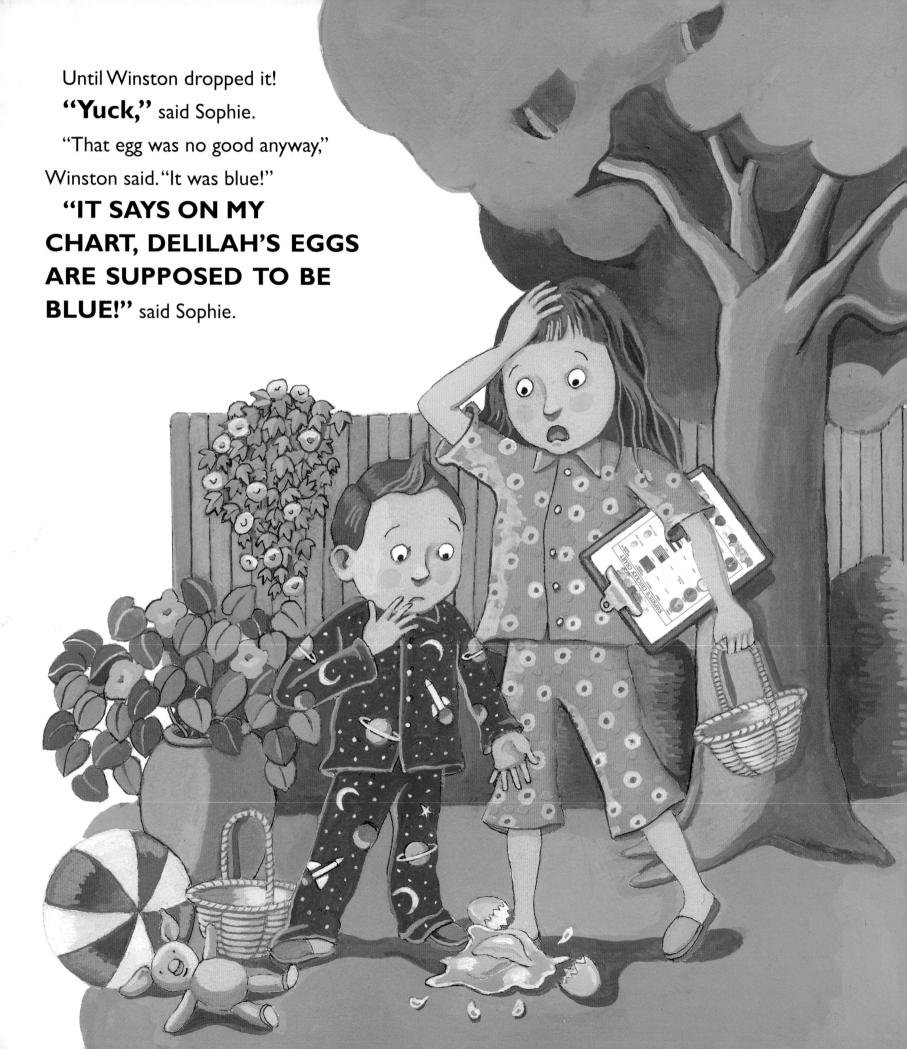

Until Winston dropped it!

"Yuck," said Sophie.

"That egg was no good anyway," Winston said. "It was blue!"

"IT SAYS ON MY CHART, DELILAH'S EGGS ARE SUPPOSED TO BE BLUE!" said Sophie.

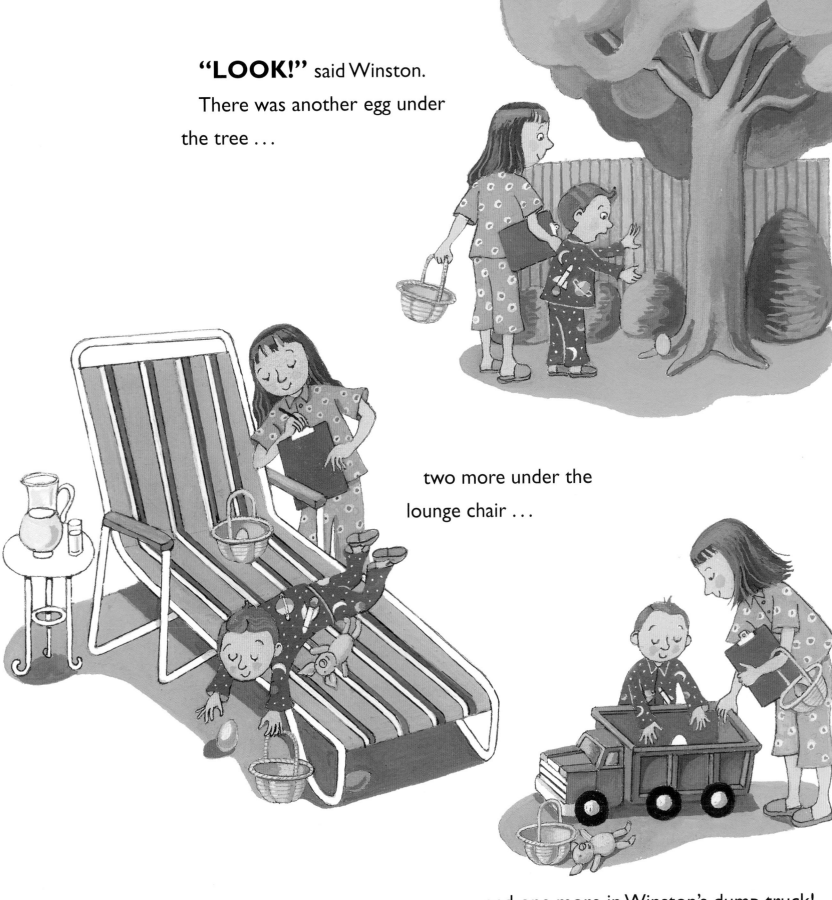

"LOOK!" said Winston.
There was another egg under the tree . . .

two more under the
lounge chair . . .

and one more in Winston's dump truck!
But then they noticed something else . . .

THE CHICKENS WERE GONE!

"OH NO!" CRIED WINSTON. "FIRST WE HAD CHICKENS WITH NO EGGS, AND NOW WE HAVE EGGS WITH NO CHICKENS!"

"Don't worry, Winston," said Sophie. "I know how to find missing chickens."

"We'll follow the trail of poop!"

It wasn't so easy.

Winston got stuck on the rosebush.
But Sophie pried him off . . .

and patched him up . . .

and they continued on . . .

Don't worry, Daphne! I'm coming!

until they reached the sliding
doors to the family room . . .

There they were—Desirée,
Daphne, Divina, Delilah, and Dawn . . .

eating leftover pizza and watching
The Deep-Sea Adventures of a Lobster Named Leonard!

That morning, everybody ate
pancakes and blueberry muffins
made with the fresh eggs.

"Hooray for the chickens!" said Daddy.

Winston gave Daphne his **WHOLE** muffin.

Then, when everyone had finished eating . . .

THEy ALL DiD THE

CHICKEN DANCE!

Buk-buk bawk!

AUTHOR'S NOTE

Thanks to all the folks in Brooklyn, New York, who introduced me to their hens and shared chicken stories and photos: Diane Bromberg and her daughters, Autumn and Kailin Hartley; Amber Ceffalio and her son, Paul; Jean Davis and her daughters, Leah, Naomi, and Simone Rosenthal; Sasha Durcan; and Leslie and Jason Platt Zolov and their sons, Isaac, Gus, and Arlo.

Backyard chicken coops have become popular in many American cities and suburbs over the last ten years. Chickens are the easiest and cheapest farm animals to raise in a backyard. And the benefits are obvious—fresh eggs. People care about where their food comes from, and if you raise your own chickens, you know how they are handled and what they are fed. Many folks also enjoy watching their chickens. Some say it's better than TV! Chickens come in different breeds, just like dogs. Different breeds lay eggs of different colors and sizes, and some breeds lay eggs more often than others, but the eggs all taste the same. Check out BackYardChickens.com and MyPetChicken.com for more information.